WHITE TAIKI

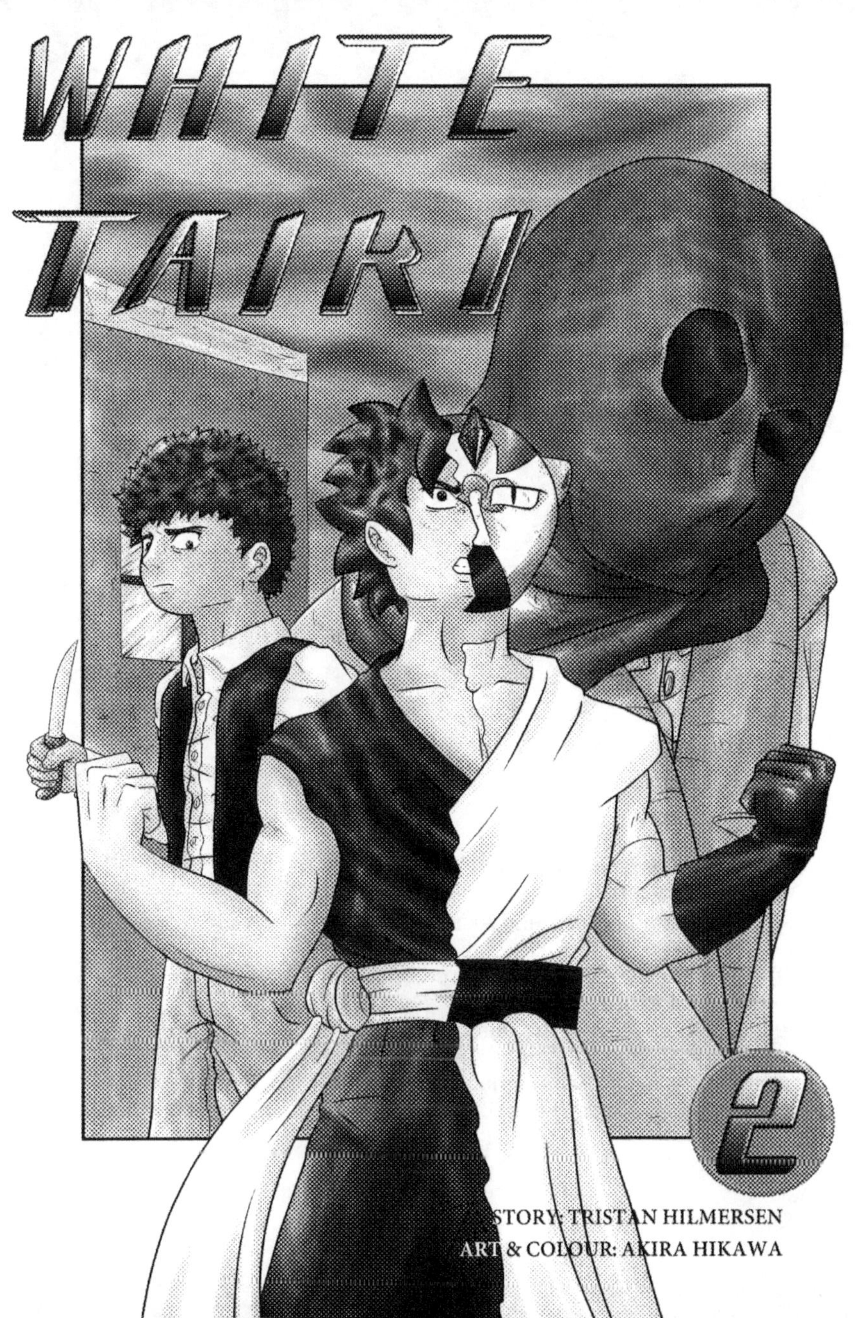

WHITE TAIKI
2
STORY: TRISTAN HILMERSEN
ART & COLOUR: AKIRA HIKAWA

WHITE TAIKI VOL. 2
CreateSpace, Charleston SC
ISBN: 9781078018814
© 2019 Tristan Hilmersen / Akira Hikawa

CHAPTER 3: THE BASTARD WITH THE BURLAP MASK

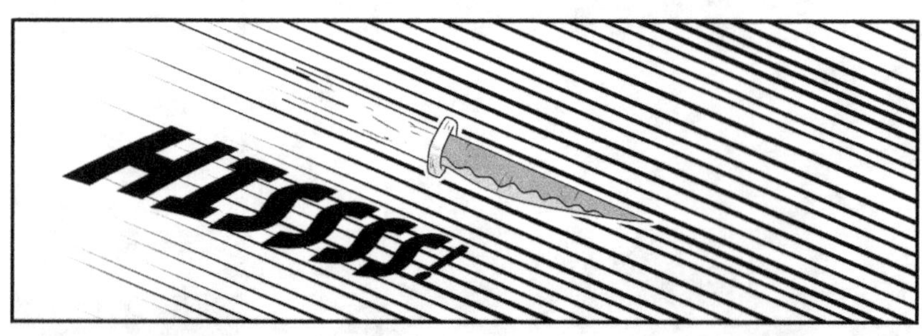
HISSSS!

CLING!

WHO THE HELL IS PLAYING MUSIC AT A TIME LIKE THIS?

ATTENTION, I'M AWARE THAT YOU ARE ALL TRYING TO FIND YOSHIKUNI TAIKI, BUT I ASSURE YOU, THAT WILL NOT BE IN YOUR BEST INTERESTS. I'M CAPABLE OF KILLING EVERYONE OF YOU, SO LISTEN UP.

WHICH ONE OF Y'ALL SICK BASTARDS PUT THAT ON THE PLAYER?

FIND WHERE THE SOUND IS COMING FROM... NOW!!!

TRUNCH!
BLOODY HELL...

ONE OF OUR MEN IS DEAD, BUT THAT'S WHAT ALL OF YOU SIGNED UP FOR! NOW, GO ARREST THIS MAN!

YES, SIR!

WHAT THE HELL ARE YOU?
I WAS GOING TO WAIT, BUT I DON'T MIND GETTING MY HANDS DIRTY.
Grab
BANG
WHAT THE HELL IS GOING ON?! I'M OUTTA HERE!

11

BANG!

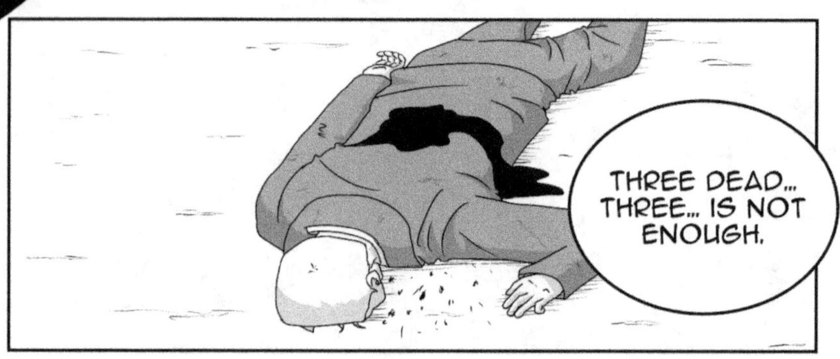

THREE DEAD...
THREE... IS NOT
ENOUGH.

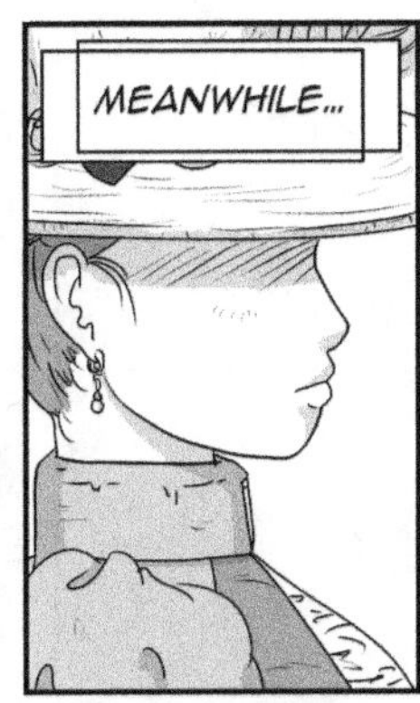
MEANWHILE...

FTP

FISH SOUP!
FISH SOUP!
GET IT WHILE
IT'S HOT!

YOU THERE,
MA'AM!

I KNOW WHO YOU ARE!

YOU WERE AN ACTRESS IN THAT MUSICAL, RIGHT?

I... DON'T KNOW.

BUT YOU DO WORK IN THOSE THEATRE PERFORMANCES.
SCRATCH
CORRECT?

I SHOULD GET GOING.

AT YOSHIKUNI'S HOUSE.

I'VE NEVER SEEN THIS DAMN MASK OR THAT JOURNAL IN MY LIFE, AND I DON'T WANT TO KNOW WHAT IT IS.

NANAMI WAS KILLED, AND I JUST WANT THIS OUT OF MY LIFE!

POF

WHY?

RUN...
RUN AWAY
AS FAST AS
YOU CAN!

WH—WHAT
ARE YOU
DOING?
GET OUT
OF HERE.

COME ON.
GET UP!

THERE'S...
THERE'S A
MONSTER
ON THE LOOSE...

GET
UP.

BANG!

22

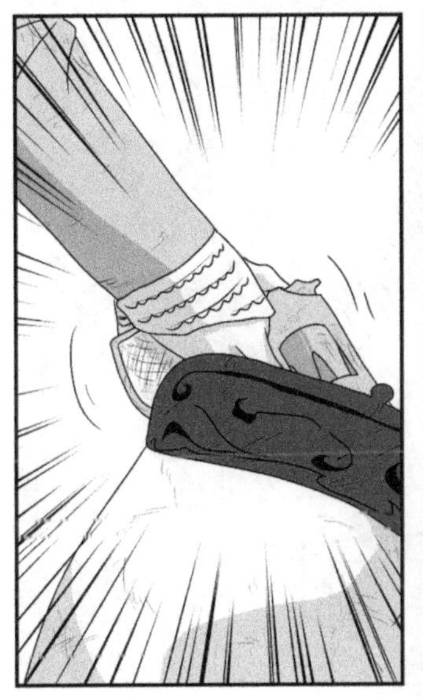

GOING SOMEWHERE?
BANG!

NICE SHOT, BUT I'M AFRAID YOU'VE MISSED. NOW...

MY TURN.

PAF!

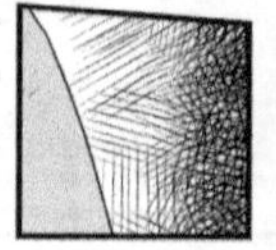

BOY, IS THERE A REASON WHY YOU ARE COVERED IN THAT RED FILTH?
SAMUEL R. WALLS, DEPUTY CHIEF OF THE CARSON CITY POLICE DIVISION.

YES.
WELL, YOU'RE GOING TO HAVE TO COME WITH ME TO THE STATION TO CLEAR SOME THINGS UP.
OKAY.

POLIC

BAAARF!

YOU'RE IN BIG TROUBLE JEB, I'VE BEEN LOOKING ALL OVER TOWN FOR Y-!

WH...
WHAT THE HELL IS GOING ON HERE??!!

YOUR SON...
IS A MONSTER.

HUH?

THAT BOY...
NEEDS TO BE BURNED AT THE STAKES LIKE THE DEMON HE IS!

JEB... YOU... DID THIS?

HE DID THIS... THAT BOY... DID ALL OF THIS!

...

GET THIS BOY OUT OF MY SIGHT...

BUT...

ARREST THIS DEMON ALREADY!

PAF!

PAF!

WOAH, GREAT HIT!

WHAT'S THAT?

HUH? OH, THAT'S THE MARKET FESTIVAL.
THIS IS THE FIRST YEAR THE TOWN STARTED DOING IT.
HAVEN'T YOU HEARD?

CLICK

STOP!

GA
RA
GASHAAN!!

YOU'RE NANAMI'S BROTHER, RIGHT?

YEAH, WHAT'S IT TO YOU?

EVERYONE RUN!!!

32

YOU WANT TO HURT THOSE PEOPLE, AND THERE'S NO WAY IN HELL THAT I'M GONNA LET THAT HAPPEN.

MOVE IT!

NEVER.

FZZZZ...
RIP!

YOU'RE NOT GETTING OUT OF MY SIGHT!

GRAB
TAP

HAVE YOU READ IT YET? THE JOURNAL?

NO. HOW DID YOU KNOW ABOUT THAT?

THERE'S AN ASSORTMENT OF THINGS YOU'D BE SURPRISED BY IN MY FATHER'S WAREHOUSE.
HUH?

GRAB

CALLING UNITS!
JEB STEVENSON
IS MISSING
IN ACTION!

FIRST ONE HOME IS A ROTTEN EGG!
ELROY PARKER, AGE 8.
BYRON CALVERT, AGE 8.
YOU'RE SO SLOW, DUDE!

ELROY: 16.
BYRON: 16.
GET THEM! THAT'S THE WHITE SAMURAI'S SON!
AND THE OTHER ONE IS THAT FREAK FROM THE SLUMS!

DAMN! I THINK WE LOST THEM!
THE WHITE SAMURAI REVEALED
HE WAS A HERO... SO, WHY IS EVERYONE MAKING HIM SEEM LIKE A VILLAIN?!
THE WHITE SAMURAI
REVEALED

CHAPTER 4: WHEN THE WOLF HOWLS AT NOON

I DON'T KNOW WHY THAT CREEP WAS SO HELLBENT ON BRINGING UP NANAMI...
BUT THE ONLY CLUE I'VE GOT IS THIS JOURNAL.
WHETHER I LIKE WHAT'S IN HERE OR NOT.
THERE'S SOMETHING I'VE GOTTA KNOW!
TO YOSHIKUNI

OUT OF ALL THE OTHERS, THERE IS ONE THAT TRULY STANDS OUT.

THIS ONE SEEMED HELPLESS AT THE START, BUT CURRENTLY HE IS THE CANDIDATE WHO SHOWS THE MOST POTENTIAL.

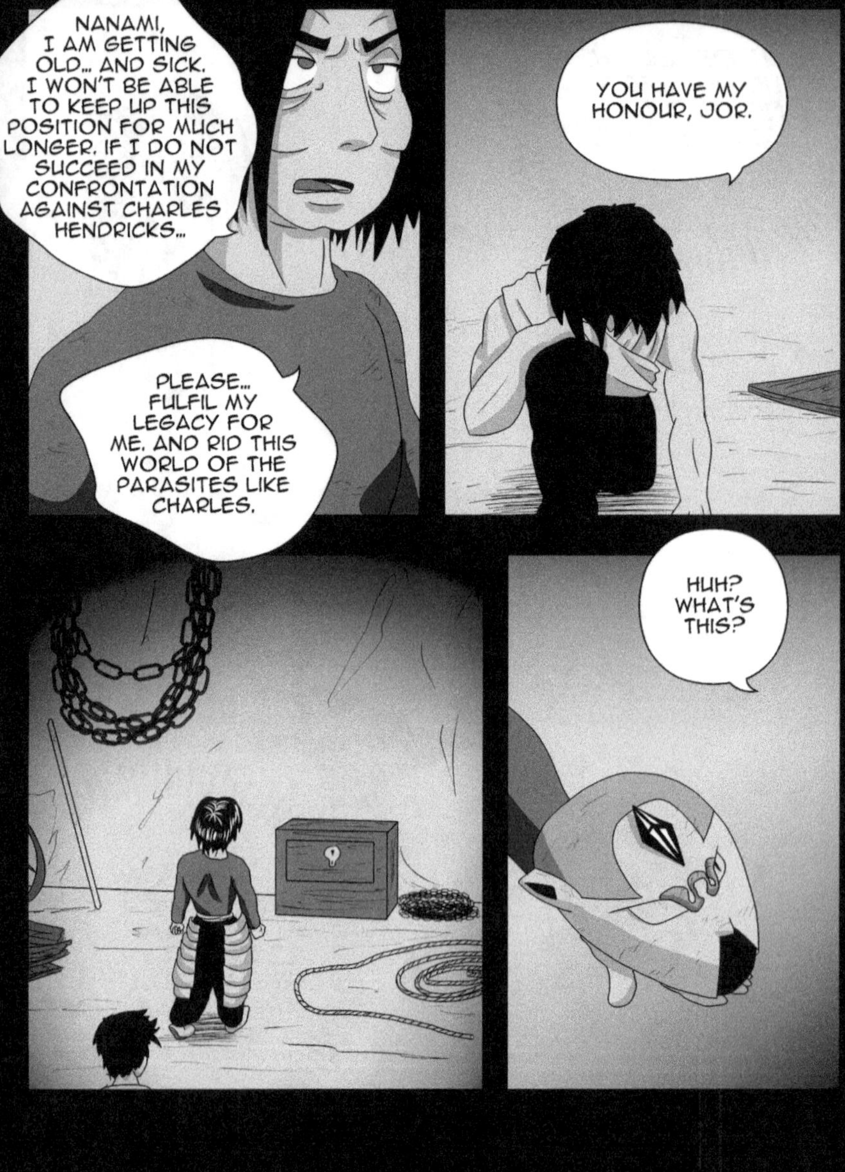

NANAMI, I AM GETTING OLD... AND SICK. I WON'T BE ABLE TO KEEP UP THIS POSITION FOR MUCH LONGER. IF I DO NOT SUCCEED IN MY CONFRONTATION AGAINST CHARLES HENDRICKS...
PLEASE... FULFIL MY LEGACY FOR ME. AND RID THIS WORLD OF THE PARASITES LIKE CHARLES.
YOU HAVE MY HONOUR, JOR.
HUH? WHAT'S THIS?

THIS MASK WAS HANDCRAFTED BY A RESPECTABLE ARMORER FROM OVERSEAS AND I WANT YOU TO HAVE IT.
BUT...
I CAN TELL THAT YOU ARE STILL AFRAID

HOW IS SOMEONE IN NEED SUPPOSED TO HAVE TRUST IN YOU IF YOUR QUIVERING MOUTH SHOWS THAT YOU ARE MORE SCARED THAN THEY ARE?
THE MASK IS NOT ONLY AN ARMOR, BUT IT IS MORE IMPORTANTLY AN ICON THAT STOPS CRIMINALS IN THEIR TRACKS, AND GIVES VICTIMS A SENSE OF HOPE.

SOME WILL SEE YOU AS THE ENEMY, BUT WHEN THAT HAPPENS REMEMBER THIS...
STOP! MY BABY! MY BABY IS STILL IN THERE!
HA
HA

YOU ARE A HERO.
TH-THANK YOU.
WEAR THIS MASK FOR THE TIME BEING. WEAR IT UNTIL YOU ARE NO LONGER AFRAID.

NANAMI
...

JUST
YOU WAIT.

THE MASKED MAN SAID SOMETHING ABOUT A WAREHOUSE.
THIS IS THE ONLY ONE I COULD FIND IN THE CITY, BUT CAN THIS REALLY BE IT? IT LOOKS COMPLETELY ABANDONED.

51

EASTERN NAUTICA APARTMENT COMPLEX, NOON. MEET US AT THE ROOF ALONE IF YOU WANT TO KEEP THE BURGLAR ALIVE.

SUI?!
ARE THERE MORE THAN ONE OF THEM? I DON'T KNOW WHAT'S GOING ON HERE, BUT I'M NOT GOING TO SIT AROUND WHILE THIS HAPPENS!

SO... WHAT YOU'RE TELLING ME IS THAT JEB NEVER CAME HOME TODAY?

NO... NOT AT ALL.
SAMUEL R. WALLS DEPUTY CHIEF OF THE CARSON CITY POLICE DEPARTMENT.

I'M NOT SURE IF YOU REALIZE THE SEVERITY OF THIS SITUATION, BUT I'D RATHER NOT BE RESPONSIBLE FOR OUR ENTIRE DEPARTMENT...
LOOKING LIKE A COMPLETE LAUGHING STOCK. OUR CHIEF AND OTHER RESPECTED OFFICERS WERE ATTACKED EARLIER TODAY.
TAP

YES, I KNOW.

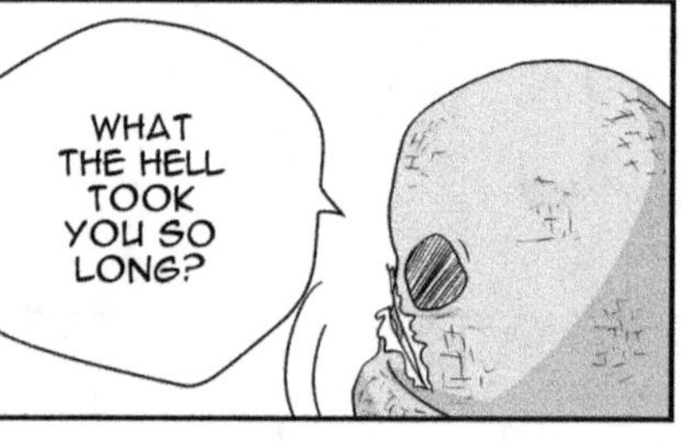

WHAT THE HELL TOOK YOU SO LONG?

I WAS SEARCHING FOR YOSHIKUNI, I'M NOT SURE IF HE'LL BE HERE.

DON'T WORRY... HE'LL SHOW.

AHA!
THE GUEST
OF HONOUR HAS
ARRIVED!

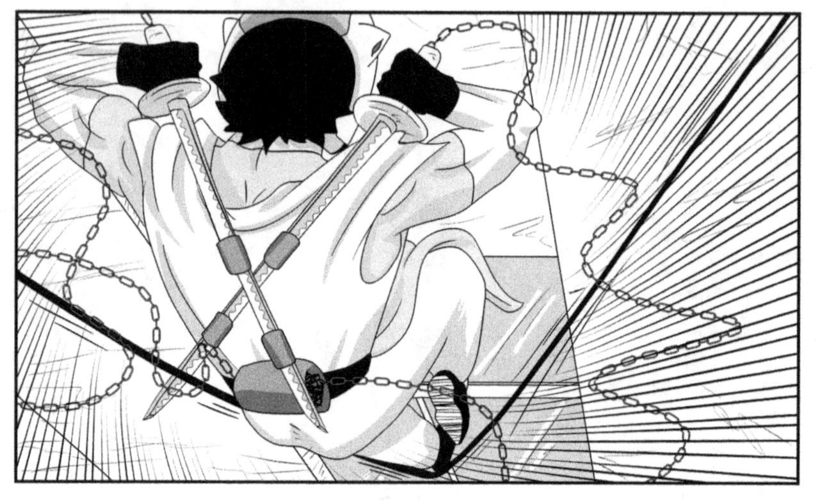

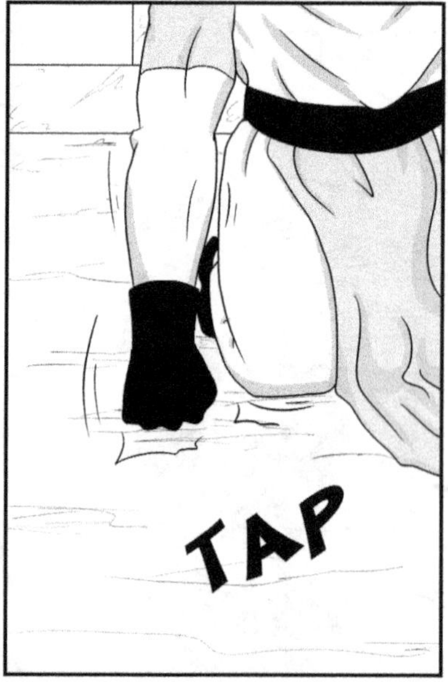

56

57

YOSHIKUNI!
I DON'T BELIEVE
WE'VE HAD A PROPER
INTRODUCTION!
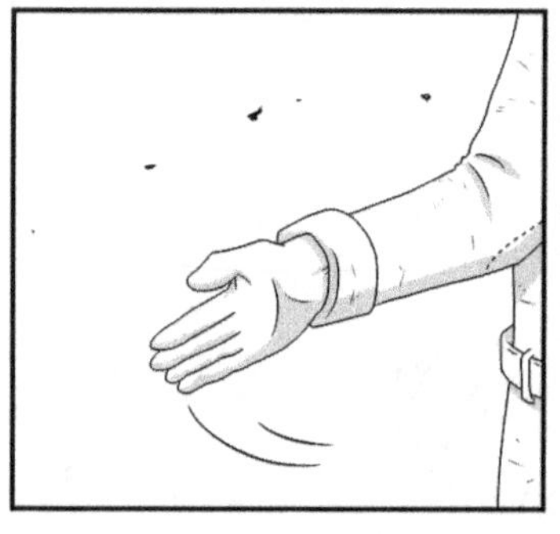

PUNCH!

HAVE YOU BEEN CAPTURED AS WELL, ELROY?
NO, I'M NOT.
SO, YOU'RE ON THIS GUY'S SIDE NOW, HUH?
I'VE BEEN ON HIS SIDE MUCH LONGER THAN I'VE BEEN ON YOURS, YOSHIKUNI.
BANG!

YOU BASTARD!

CHIN!

HHHSSS

WHERE'S SUI?
OH, THIS MIGHT NOT BE THE BEST TIME TO TELL YOU THIS...
BUT SHE IS ACTUALLY IN A STORAGE ROOM SOMEWHERE IN THE BUILDING.

DAMMIT!

WHAT THE? IT WON'T BUDGE!
CLAC
CLAC

I ALSO HAVE THE KEY TO THE DOOR.

CHIN!
YOU REALLY KNOW HOW TO PISS ME OFF, YOU KNOW?!
CLICK
CLICK!

EMPTY...

KLONK!

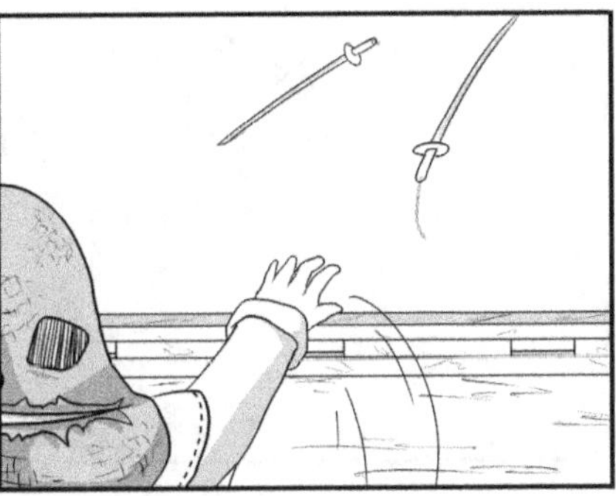

KLANK!
I HAVE A BAD FEELING ABOUT THIS.

GRAB!

I SUPPOSE THE BLADED ASSASSIN ENDS NOW.
BLADED ASSASSIN, HUH?
NAH, THAT DOESN'T HAVE THE SAME RING THAT IT USED TO...

MAYBE IT'S TIME FOR A CHANGE... LIKE THE WHITE TAIKI... YEAH, THAT SOUNDS ABOUT RIGHT.
THE WHITE TAIKI.

YOU MADE A COMPLETE MOCKERY OF MYSELF AS WELL AS MY FATHER. I AM BYRON CALVERT, SON OF THE WHITE SAMURAI.

!

GRAB

LET GO!

ZAS

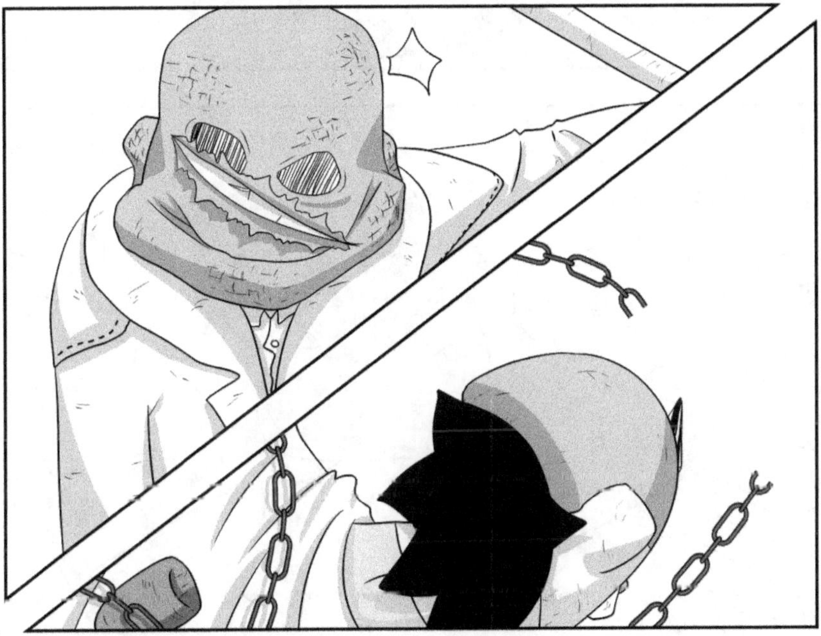

BYRON!
YOSHIKUNI!

PUNCH

IS THIS
SOME KIND
OF JOKE?! NO...
HIS MANNERISMS...
EVERYTHING ABOUT
THIS GUY... REMINDS
OF THE WHITE
SAMURAI!

RAS!
MY HEAD FEELS LIKE IT'S SPINNING A MILLION MILES PER HOUR!
I'VE GOTTA PAY ATTENTION... GOTTA FOCUS!!!

RIGHT NOW... MY BLOOD IS BOILING...
PAFF!

CRICK

BUT I'VE GOTTA GIVE THIS MY ALL!

AAAAGHH!!!

GRAB

PUNCH!
PUNCH!
THERE'S NO TURNING BACK NOW!

ENOUGH!!!

I DON'T MEAN TO SPOIL THE MOMENT HERE, BUT YOU WILL ALMOST CERTAINLY DIE IF YOU HIT THE TREES LIKE THAT. I'D PERSONALLY SUGGEST SPREADING YOUR BODY OUT TO DAMPEN THE IMPACT.

PAF!
CRAC!
SCRATCH!
PAM!
CRAC!

FFFF---
PAF!

AH...
AH...
AH...
AH...

QUITE THE LONG FALL, EH? THERE SHOULD REALLY BE SOME TYPE OF RAILING ON THAT CLIFF, BECAUSE THAT THING IS NOT SAFE.

HAND OVER THE... HUFF... HUFF... KEY.

KEY? HMMM LET ME THINK OF WHERE I PUT THAT THING...
OH, NOW I REMEMBER ...

ELROY HAD THE REAL KEY THE ENTIRE TIME!

YOU... HUFF... HUFF...
I AM WHAT?
YOU MAKE ME SICK TO MY STO-MACH!!!
Y'KNOW WHEN I WAS YOUNGER I USED TO WALK ALONGSIDE A RIVER BANK.

I'D PUT ONE FOOT IN FRONT OF THE OTHER AND WALK THAT WAY TO SCHOOL EVERYDAY OVER THE COURSE OF A FEW MONTHS.
UNFORTUNATELY THOUGH, ONE DAY DURING WINTER TIME, I LOST MY BALANCE AND FELL INTO THE FREEZING COLD WATER.

THIS RESULTED IN MYSELF GETTING A NASTY FEVER AND A CASE OF PNEUMONIA WHICH ALMOST KILLED ME.

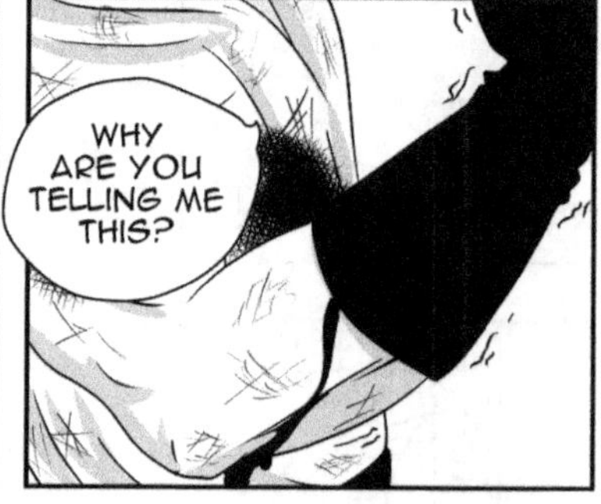

WHY ARE YOU TELLING ME THIS?

BECAUSE NOW THAT I THINK ABOUT IT...
THIS RIVER LOOKS AN AWFUL LOT LIKE IT.

SLAM!

WE HAVE
TO GO!

WIGGLE

THAT FALL IS FINALLY STARTING TO TAKE A TOLL ON YOU, HUH?
DOESN'T SURPRISE ME. I'M GETTING PRETTY SORE MYSELF.

EXPLAIN TO ME... HUFF... HOW YOU MANAGED... TO GET... THIS FAR.
YOU WANT TO KNOW MY PLAN?

YIAAAA!!!

PAF!
SPLASH!
ARE YOU GONNA GET IT? OR DOES WHITE SAMURAI JUNIOR NOT WANT TO GET SICK?

HAHAHA HAHAHA!!!

I SUPPOSE I CAN TELL YOU WHAT HAPPENED BEHIND THE SCENES. AFTERALL, THERE REALLY ISN'T MUCH TO SAY.

WHAT DO YOU MEAN?
HAVE YOU HEARD OF THE COP KILLER JEB STEVENSON?
MORE OR LESS.

WELL, JEB WASN'T INVOLVED WHATSOEVER. HE WAS JUST A CLUELESS KID KNOWN FOR SOME MINOR OFFENSES THAT HAPPENED TO BE WALKING BY AT THE WRONG TIME.

YOU... HUFF... HUFF... SPINELESS COWARD.

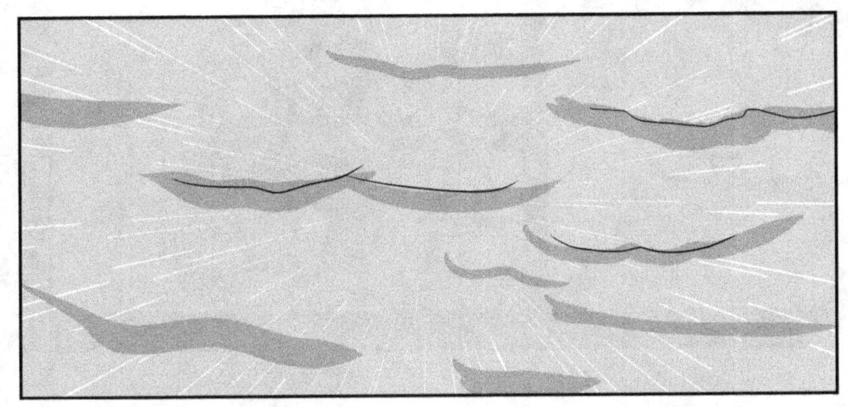

YOU
FEEL
THAT?

HELP!
FUNCH!
HELP ME!
PLIC

Y...
YOU'RE...
ARE YOU GONNA LET PEOPLE LIKE THAT PICK ON YOU FOR THE REST OF YOUR LIFE?
THANKS A LOT BUT... MY ONLY SKILL IS MY UNCANNY ABILITY TO LOSE.
I'M NOT A FIGHTER THOUGH, THAT'S FOR SURE.

YOU'RE NOT GETTING OFF THAT EASY, NOW. YOUR PAYMENT FOR ME SAVING YOU IS THAT YOU HAVE TO TRAIN WITH ME UNTIL YOU CAN BEAT THOSE GUYS TO A PULP.
I DON'T KNOW ABOUT ALL THAT, BUT I GUESS I OWE YOU MY LIFE.

IT'S ONLY A MATTER OF TIME BEFORE ONE OF US LOSES ALL STRENGTH AND DIES HERE.

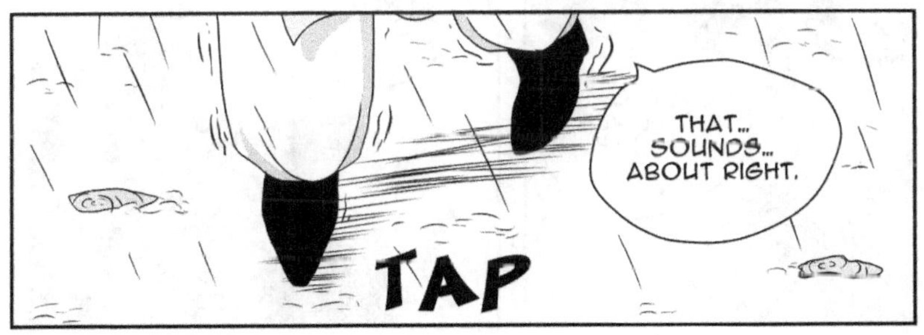

THAT... SOUNDS... ABOUT RIGHT.
TAP

HE'S RIGHT. I'M NEVER GOING TO BEAT HIM THROWING A BUNCH OF WEAK PUNCHES.
MY BEST BET IS TO PUT ALL MY REMAINING STRENGTH INTO ONE LAST PUNCH.
SHAAAA
HAVE YOU GIVEN UP YET?

NOT QUITE.

ZAS

PUNCH!

WIGGLE

PAF!

PAF!

STEP AWAY FROM HIM, MA'AM!

2 DAYS LATER.

COME
HOME,
KID

WE'RE GLAD YOU'RE AWAKE...

MR. TAIKI.

FEH... I GUESS HAVING A DEATH WISH RUNS IN THE FAMILY.
END OF TOME 2

CONCEPT ART

WHITE TAIKI

BYRON

JEB

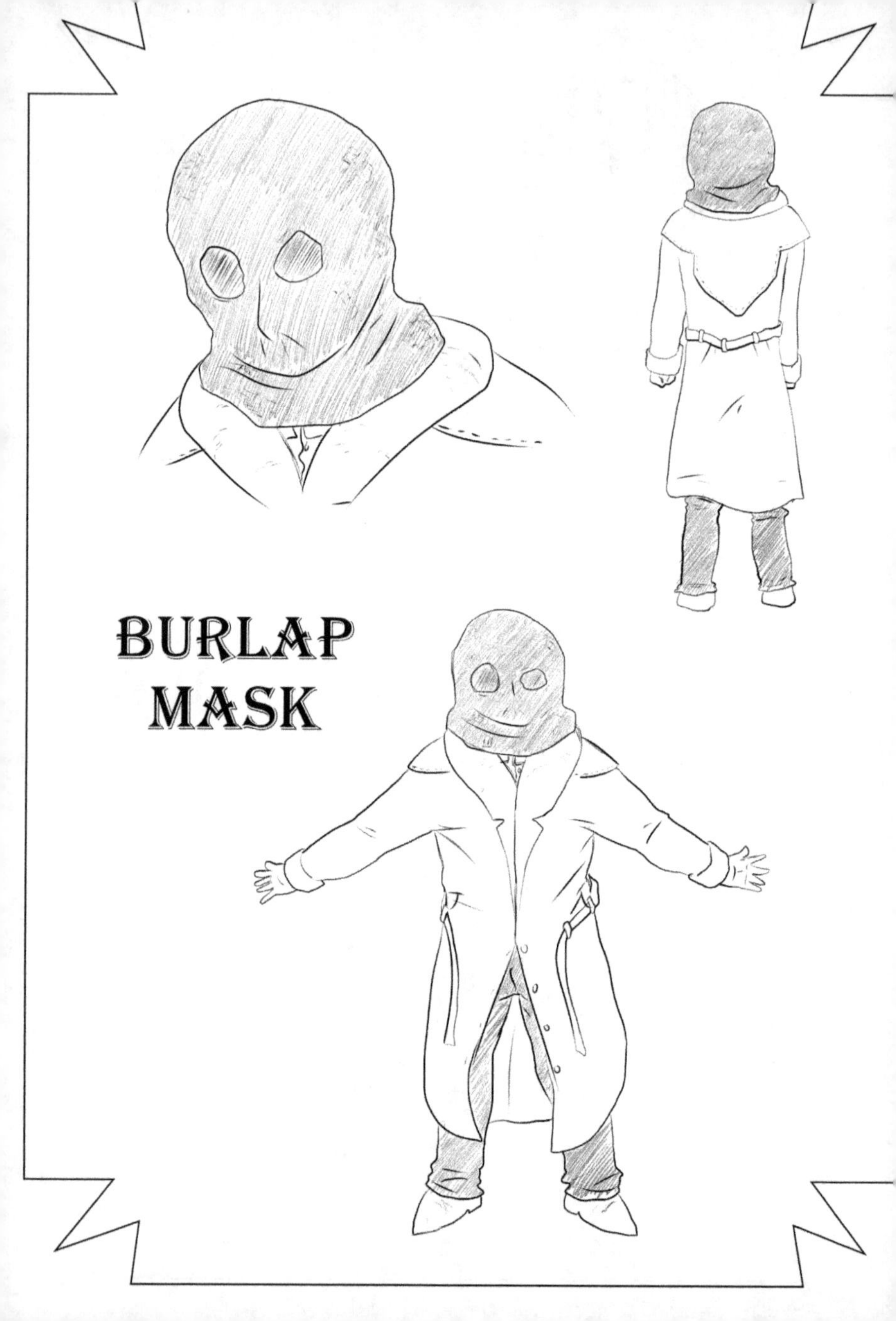

BURLAP
MASK

ELROY
(URCHIN)

White Taiki Volume 2 Interview

Interview by former University of Georgia professor, Sayed S. Ahmed

Questions for Tristan Hilmersen (Author)

Q: How do you feel after the release of volume 2 of White Taiki?

A: I'm glad that it's finished and that people are going to have more White Taiki content to read, because comic series are usually more enjoyable when there's more of a complete story to read.

Q. How do you compare your experience about volume 1 and volume 2 of White Taiki?

A: Volume 2 was a slow production at the start, because I was writing a few very different versions of the script, but once I wrote the last draft and once Akira got used to drawing more of the characters, the comic was coming together at a good speed. I also have a much more clear direction of where I want the end of the series to go now.

Q. What kind of thrill and suspense we can expect in the third volume of the graphic novel?

A: Readers can expect more development on Yoshikuni's character arc, as well as a pretty crazy final fight.

Q. In a YouTube video, you said that White Taiki can be called a graphic novel or a manga, but primarily you preferred to call it 'a western comic but highly influenced by Japanese manga.' Please explain this statement.

A: It's kind of a mix overall, and since volume 2 is done now it's hard to put one main classification on it, but readers can call it whatever they want.

Q. How important is the illustration for a graphic novel? Please make some comments on the illustration of Akira Hikawa.

A: The artwork is very important for White Taiki, because it's a pretty fast paced story for the most part, so it wouldn't work as well if it were a novel with only text, because a lot of the story would end up being descriptions. Also, since what a character is feeling in a scene is very important, the drawings greatly help add tone with the characters' facial expressions, and Akira has done a great job with that.

Q. What is your future project?

A: I've had a sci-fi story in mind for several years now, and it's going to be pretty different from White Taiki, because it'll have a lot of comedic and light hearted moments, while still having an overarching villain, so that'll most likely be my next series after I finish White Taiki.

Q: As the illustrator of the White Taiki, how is your experience different in Vol 2 than in Vol 1?

A: For the first tome I showed a more realistic, objective face of the American Western and the world of samurais. However, in the second tome I should say that a more conceptual style was used, where the scenes are told from the character himself, more personal, and we can feel much better their feelings and fears.

Q: In a wordpress blog, you define yourself as a "comic artist, illustrator, concept artist"---all three creative identities. Which identity suits you best?

A: I guess I cannot choose one of them only, because in my working style one is nothing without the others. Let's say that concept art lets open my mind and pour over the paper everything there is inside. Thanks to illustration I can try new techniques, so it's always fun and very interesting -and relaxing-. And making comics is the best way to tell things — I can express anything I want, play with the reader and show a lot of elements and points of view that cannot be shown through a simple drawing.

Q: Do you have any plan for experimentation on the illustration in White Taiki Vol 3?

A: Sure. I'm always experimenting. I have fun trying different styles and techniques, and as for tome 3, I'll bring along great innovations and new ways to express what happens in the story.

Q: In twitter profile, you are " occasionally funny, often sequential, always graphic". Could you please explain such a beautiful self-description?

A: White Taiki is a serious graphic novel, there's no room for humour. But this is not my sole creation, I also have other mangas in a completely different universe and sometimes with a touch of humour, like Anecdomics or The New Trend. But above all, the way I try to show my creativity is drawing, and that can be a sequential art -my favourite style-, an illustration or a concept art.

Q: As the illustrator, how do you evaluate the role of the script of White Taiki?

A: I think that Tristan does a great job with the script. I am a storyteller myself too, and it is not easy to create a story from nothing — storytelling must be treated with a lot of care if you want to surprise the reader and catch all their attention throughout the story.

Q: Say something about your future project.

A: Once White Taiki is finished, I would like to keep on the story of Gods, an unfinished manga I started a few years ago, and after that I'll start a new project in a whole new context, and I'm only saying that it will be something different from what I usually draw, which is people or monsters...

TRISTAN HILMERSEN

As a half Norwegian from the U.S., Tristan enjoys working on a variety of creative projects such as writing comic books and making reviews in addition to being a big fan of comics, manga, and movies.

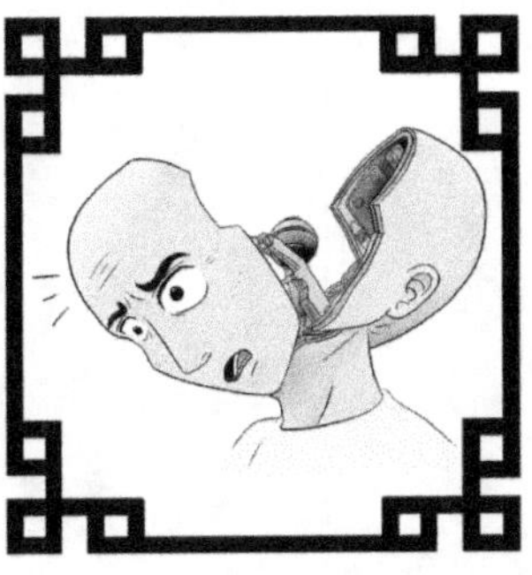

AKIRA HIKAWA

This comic artist lives now in Palma de Mallorca. Besides working on the saga *White Taiki*, he created other mangas like *Gods* or *Anecdomics*, he is member of *Dibuhunters Fanzine* and collaborator in a radio program about TV series.

WHITE TAIKI